THE GIFT OF
MINDFULNESS

365 Short Stories, Zen Quotes, Meditations, and Daily Reflections for **Inner Peace & Happiness**

KAI TSUKIMI

*We'd like to dedicate this page to the readers who supported the campaign to raise funds for the **Mindful Life Project**. Whether through encouragement, generosity, or by sharing copies during the book's launch, your presence made a meaningful difference.*

David - Nanaimo, BC, Canada

Anthony - Indianapolis, Indiana, USA

Bethany - New York, New York, USA

Shelley - Toronto, Ontario, Canada

Darcy - Ashburn, Virginia, USA

Lisa - New York, New York, USA

Annie - Los Angeles, California, USA

Askim - Dallas, Texas, USA

Kevin - Los Angeles, California, USA

A FREE GIFT FOR READERS 🌿

A book can shift your perspective, but a ritual can transform your life. As a thank-you for reading, I'd like to offer you our exclusive Zen Clarity Kit; designed to help you clear your mind, refocus, and make Zen teachings a part of your daily routine.

WHAT'S INSIDE THE KIT?

✓ **The Zen Morning Ritual Guide** – A simple daily practice to anchor your mind in stillness.

✓ **A 5-Minute Audio Meditation** – Gently guide yourself into a state of clarity and focus.

✓ **Zen Minimalism Wallpapers** – Subtle reminders to cultivate presence throughout your day.

>> Scan the QR Code or click here to download your free gift <<

INTRODUCTION

The Gift of Mindfulness

When did you first notice you were *here*?

Not just alive, but aware. Watching your breath. Sensing the wind. Realizing that behind the thoughts, there is someone watching them.

Maybe it was when you were two. Or four. Or six. Maybe you're only just noticing this now—or maybe it happens every morning, if only for a breath.

Consciousness is a mystery and a miracle. Of all the beings that roam the earth, only humans can step back and witness their own minds. Only we can ask, *Why am I thinking this? Why did I react that way? What if I chose something else?*

This ability—to pause, to observe, to choose—is mindfulness.

And mindfulness is a gift. A quiet one. Easily forgotten. Easily remembered.

This book is a reminder.

What's Inside?

The Gift of Mindfulness offers 365 daily invitations to return to presence.

- ✓ **Short Zen Stories** – Readable in under two minutes, these tales open a door to insight, confusion, or wonder.

- ✓ **Zen Quotes** – Timeless words from teachers old and new, meant not to inform, but to awaken.

- ✓ **Guided Meditations** – Simple breathing practices to ground you in your body and the moment.

- ✓ **Reflection Prompts** – Questions to ponder after the story has ended... or perhaps just begun.

- ✓ **Silent Days** – A word. An image. Nothing more. No answers. Just space to feel and see what arises.

There is no commentary, no conclusions. Only threads. You choose which ones to follow.

How to Read This Book

There is no right way.

You may start on page one and continue through the year. You may flip to any page that calls to you and read just that. You may keep it on your bedside or by your tea—something to turn to when the noise gets loud.

Some days the story will speak to you. Some days, it won't. That's all right. Zen is not about always feeling peaceful. It's about being awake to whatever is here.

So come as you are.

With your questions, your restlessness, your hope, or your tired eyes.

One page a day. Or none. Or ten.

This is your gift. Use it how you will.

Now breathe. Turn the page. And see what waits in the stillness.

January

THE GHOST AND THE BEANS

EACH NIGHT, after the rice had been rinsed and the lamp lit, she returned.

Not quite a shadow, not quite a voice—just the sense of her, bustling around the kitchen, humming off-key. She spoke as she always had, asking about the day's weather, the neighbors' dog, the crack in the water jar. Her presence was so familiar, the man didn't question it. Why would he? He missed her less when she was there.

Still, something clung to the corners of the room—some ache that even her laughter didn't clear.

One night, he sat at the table with a bowl of beans and said softly, "If you know everything as you used to, tell me—how many beans are in my hand?"

Silence. Then a breeze, like someone quietly leaving.

She never returned.

REFLECTION

In what ways do you avoid silence, even when you're alone?

____

____

____

____

ZEN QUOTE

 When you realize nothing is lacking, the whole world belongs to you.

LAO TZU

THE SOUND OF THE BELL

A student asked the master, "How do I awaken?"

The master led him to the bell tower.

"Strike it," he said.

The student tapped the side of the great bronze bell. A faint chime wavered in the air, then disappeared like a shy thought.

"Again."

This time the student struck harder. A deeper tone rang out, lingering a little longer.

"Again."

With both hands, the student swung the mallet full force. The bell sang, clear and endless. The sound rolled through the valley, touched the trees, stirred the crows from their perches.

The master nodded. "Some truths only echo. Others resound."

He turned and walked away.

The bell was still singing.

*When in your life did you finally give something your full effort—
and what was the result?*

____

____

____

____

ZEN QUOTE

Each morning, we are born again. What we do today is what matters most.

BUDDHA

MEDITATION: THE STILL WATER

Type: Visualization

Theme: Calm, clarity

Imagine a still lake in the early morning.

The surface is smooth like glass.

You sit nearby, and your breath begins to slow.

Each inhale is like a ripple.

Each exhale, the ripple fades.

You don't need to change anything.

Just watch and breathe.

Let your thoughts flow like leaves across the surface of the water.

The lake holds everything—without resistance.

Sit with this stillness for a few minutes.

Let it stay with you.

BOOKS INTO FIRE

When the scholar finally understood, he closed the last book without a sound.

He looked around his study—shelves bowing under years of ink and effort, the sacred texts, the commentaries on commentaries, the careful footnotes written in candlelight.

He carried them out one by one, stacking them in the courtyard like offerings. The neighbors gathered. Some thought it was madness. Others thought it was a ceremony.

He lit the match.

The fire caught quickly, as if the books had been waiting. Pages curled into smoke. Letters danced upward, unread and unneeded.

He watched without blinking.

When the last flame died, the wind came and took the ashes.

He did not write again.

REFLECTION

What parts of your identity are built on things you've been taught, but never questioned?

____

____

____

____

ZEN QUOTE

Only when you can be extremely pliable and soft can you be extremely hard and strong.

ZEN PROVERB

TWO RABBITS

The student had been running for days—back and forth between two teachers, two temples, two paths.

One offered silence, the other scripture. One served tea, the other served questions. He loved them both, and learned from both, but the more he tried to follow each, the more tangled his feet became.

One morning, he arrived late to the first master's gate, dust in his hair and breath uneven.

"I've been with the other teacher," he confessed. "I hoped to learn more —faster."

The master looked out over the fields.

"A hunter," he said, "who chases two rabbits... catches none."

Nothing more.

The student bowed. But he didn't move.

REFLECTION

What's one commitment in your life that feels divided? What would it mean to choose?

ZEN QUOTE

Zen is not some kind of excitement, but concentration on our usual everyday routine.

SHUNRYU SUZUKI

THE STRAWBERRY

A man was running from a tiger.

He raced through the trees, heart pounding, until he came to the edge of a cliff. Without thinking, he leapt, and caught a vine halfway down.

Above him, the tiger paced. Below, another waited.

Then he noticed two mice, one white and one black, gnawing at the vine.

He hung there, breathless, suspended between the two tigers and the slow work of teeth.

Just beside him, a wild strawberry grew from the cliffside—small, red, and impossibly perfect.

He reached out, plucked it, and placed it on his tongue.

How sweet it was.

REFLECTION

What is your "strawberry" right now—small, fleeting, and easy to miss if you don't pause?

____

____

____

____

 Smile, breathe and go slowly.

THICH NHAT HANH

MINDFUL MOMENTS

Touch the earth
Cool soil. Warm sun. A quiet hello from below.

THE PRICE OF THE CAT'S HEAD

"What is the most valuable thing in the world?" the student asked.

The master didn't answer. He walked into the garden, bent down, and returned holding something in a cloth.

He opened it.

Inside was the severed head of a cat, sun-bleached and long dead. Its eyes were hollow. Its jaw frozen mid-yawn or mid-scream—it was hard to tell.

The student recoiled. "Why that?"

The master said, "Because no one can name its price."

He wrapped it again and left it on the table.

breathe

REFLECTION

How do you react when you're shown something you don't understand?

____

____

____

____

ZEN QUOTE

Let go, or be dragged.

ZEN PROVERB

MEDITATION: ONE KIND BREATH

Type: Breath Anchor

Theme: Self-compassion

Take one slow breath in.

Imagine that breath filling you with kindness.

Let it move through your chest, your arms, your hands.

Then breathe out, gently.

Let that kindness soften the space around you.

There's nothing you need to fix.

This moment is enough.

Take another breath.

And another.

Breathe like this for a minute or two.

Then carry this kindness with you for the rest of the day.

A BEAUTIFUL CUP

There was a crash in the night.

The young monk stood frozen, a few ceramic shards at his feet, and the handle of the master's favorite tea cup still in his hand.

In the morning, he approached the master with eyes lowered.

"Why must there be death?" he asked.

The master looked up from his sweeping. "Death comes to all things," he said, "to flowers, to people... and to cups."

"But it was so beautiful."

"It still is," the master said, glancing at the broken pieces on the altar where the monk had placed them.

Then he poured tea into a different cup, as if nothing had been lost at all.

REFLECTION

What's something you lost that still feels beautiful to you, even in memory or pieces?

____

____

____

____

ZEN QUOTE

> If you are depressed, you are living in the past. If you are
> anxious, you are living in the future. If you are at peace,
> you are living in the present.

LAO TZU

THE EMPTY GIFT

A young warrior, famous for his temper, stormed into the old master's courtyard.

He spat on the stones, cursed the lineage, and called the master a fraud, a coward, a relic.

The master sat unmoved, sipping his tea.

Finally, the warrior shouted, "Do you hear me, old man? What kind of teacher are you, that you don't even defend yourself?"

The master looked up.

"If someone offers you a gift," he said, "and you do not accept it... to whom does the gift belong?"

The warrior opened his mouth, then closed it.

He left with everything he came with.

What kinds of "gifts" do people try to give you—through words or actions—that you'd be better off not taking?

____

____

____

____

ZEN QUOTE

Old friends pass away, new friends appear… The important thing is to make it meaningful: a meaningful friend – or a meaningful day.

DALAI LAMA

MINDFUL MOMENTS

Notice three sounds
Far, near, and in-between. What do you hear when you're not trying?

rest

February

THE LISTENING BOWL

THE STUDENT ENTERED the master's quarters with a bow that was just slightly too deep.

"I have seen through it all," he announced. "No self, no Buddha, no mind. There is no giver, no receiver, no path and no arrival. Emptiness flows through everything. There is nothing to attain."

The master smoked his pipe without looking up.

The student waited, certain this silence was acknowledgment.

Then, without a word, the master struck him hard across the back with the bamboo pipe.

The student yelped, startled and angry. "Why did you—?"

"If nothing exists," the master said, tapping the pipe against the bowl, "where did that come from?"

The bowl sang. The student didn't.

REFLECTION

Where do your reactions come from—especially when something touches a nerve?

____

____

____

____

ZEN QUOTE

 When you do something, you should burn yourself up completely… leaving no trace of yourself.

SHUNRYU SUZUKI

MEDITATION: WHAT IS HERE NOW?

Type: Inner Inquiry

Theme: Presence

Close your eyes for a moment.

Gently ask yourself: *What is here now?*

Don't rush to answer.

Just listen to what comes up.

Maybe it's the hum of a fan. The chirp of a bird.

Or the quiet warmth of your clothes.

Whatever it is, let it be enough.

There is wisdom in simply noticing.

Spend a few moments in this space.

Let yourself be with what is.

THE PAINTED TIGER

"For three nights," the student said, "a tiger chases me through my dreams. I run, I hide, I wake up sweating. I never see its face."

The master listened, then pointed to the blank wall of the meditation hall.

"Paint it."

The student returned the next morning with ink-stained hands and a tiger—wild-eyed and mid-pounce—stretching across the plaster. It looked ready to leap.

"Now step inside," said the master.

The student hesitated.

"Dream or waking," said the master, "you're still running."

The ink tiger stared back, unmoving.

REFLECTION

If you painted your fear on a wall, what would it look like? Could you face it?

____

____

____

____

ZEN QUOTE

 Do not follow the idea of others, but learn to listen to the voice within yourself.

DŌGEN ZENJI

RYONEN'S MIRROR

Ryonen was known for her beauty—so much so that every temple turned her away.

"Too many minds will follow your face," they said. "No monk will hear the Dharma if you speak it."

So she returned home, heated a flat iron, and pressed it to her skin.

When she returned, her cheek was scarred, her beauty gone.

The master looked at her closely and said, "Now we can begin."

Years later, Ryonen wrote:

"This body is a lamp— beautiful or not, it still burns out."

She kept a mirror on her altar, but never looked into it.

REFLECTION

What part of your identity are you most attached to—and how might it be holding you back?

____

____

____

____

return

ZEN QUOTE

 The practice of Zen is forgetting the self in the act of uniting with something.

KOUN YAMADA

MINDFUL MOMENTS

Walk slowly

Feel your foot kiss the ground. Even the air waits for you.

THE THIEF AND THE BOWL

The saint lived beneath a tree, owning nothing but a golden begging bowl—a gift from a grateful king.

One night, a thief crept through the brush and found him sitting, eyes closed, the bowl beside him.

Without opening his eyes, the saint said, "Take it."

The thief froze.

"It's heavy for someone like you," the saint added, "but you may grow strong enough to carry it."

The thief snatched the bowl and ran.

In the morning, the saint sat in the same spot, humming.

By dusk, the thief returned. He set the bowl down carefully and bowed low.

"Keep it," said the saint, smiling. "You've already brought it back."

REFLECTION

What do you carry that's too heavy now, but might teach you strength later?

____

____

____

____

ZEN QUOTE

To follow the path, look to the master, follow the master, walk with the master, see through the master, become the master.

ZEN PROVERB

MEDITATION: THE CANDLE FLAME

Type: Visualization

Theme: Focus, steadiness

Imagine a single candle burning in front of you.

Its flame dances gently but never wavers.

It glows with warmth, calm, and quiet strength.

With each breath, your body softens.

With each exhale, your mind settles.

The flame remains steady—just like you.

Let your attention rest with it.

Sit with this image for a few minutes.

Let its steadiness become yours.

YOU ARE THE MESSENGER

The teacher became famous.

People traveled across oceans to hear her speak. They quoted her in books, posted her words over sunrise photos, and bowed a little too deeply when she entered the room.

One evening, after a talk, a student asked, "When did you realize you were enlightened?"

The teacher laughed.

"Have you ever seen a letter fall in love with the envelope?"

The student blinked.

She continued, "If a message reaches you, be grateful. But don't mistake the envelope for the truth."

She left the room. No one followed.

REFLECTION

Are you waiting for a teacher to arrive... or have the teachings already reached you?

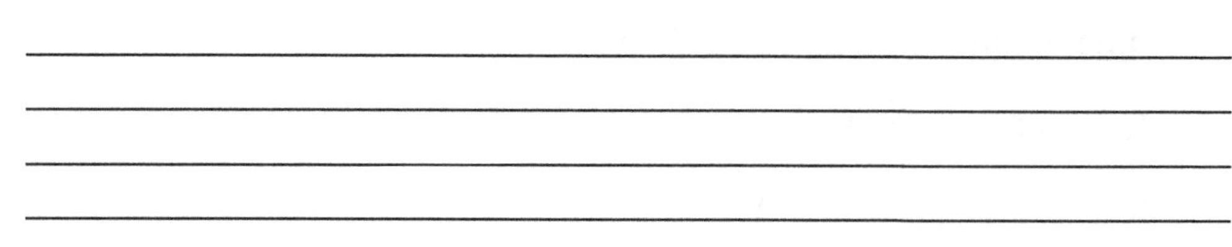

ZEN QUOTE

> Sitting quietly, doing nothing, spring comes, and the grass grows by itself.

ZEN PROVERB

THE TEA OF THE PEASANT

A nobleman invited a circle of tea connoisseurs to sample a rare and exquisite brew.

The guests sniffed, swirled, and sipped with solemn reverence. "One detects spring rain," said one. "Hints of plum blossom," said another. "A rare leaf indeed," said a third, closing his eyes.

The nobleman smiled and called for the servant.

"Tell them," he said, "where this tea came from."

The servant bowed. "It's the same blend the farmer drinks after he milks the goats. Three coins a bag."

No one spoke.

Only one guest poured himself a second cup.

REFLECTION

____

____

____

____

ZEN QUOTE

When walking, walk. When eating, eat.

ZEN PROVERB

THE WEIGHT OF HAIR

A novice stood before the mirror, hesitant.

His head was half-shaved. The other half still held the weight of childhood, style, self.

"Why must I shave it all?" he asked.

The master ran a hand over his own smooth scalp. "You don't know how much your hair weighs," he said, "until it's gone."

The novice looked down at the clippings on the floor.

They didn't look heavy.

But his head already felt lighter.

REFLECTION

If you let go of an old part of yourself, what space might open up?

____

____

____

____

ZEN QUOTE

In the beginner's mind there are many possibilities, but in the expert's there are few.

SHUNRYU SUZUKI

MINDFUL MOMENTS

Take one deep breath

Let it fill your chest like a wave. Let it leave without clinging.

THE LAND OF SATISFACTION

At the edge of a quiet road stood a wooden sign:

"This land will be given to anyone who is truly satisfied."

Many passed it by, curious but doubtful.

One man stopped, read it twice, and knocked at the nearby farmhouse.

"I am content," he said. "I want nothing. I need nothing. I have no desire but this moment. I am truly satisfied."

The farmer looked him over, nodded slowly, and said,

"Then why are you asking for land?"

The man stood there a long time, unsure of what to say.

Then he walked away.

Smiling.

REFLECTION

If you truly had everything you needed, what would you stop chasing?

____

____

____

____

ZEN QUOTE

Be master of mind rather than mastered by mind.

ZEN PROVERB

MEDITATION: ONLY THIS BREATH

Type: Breath Anchor

Theme: Simplicity, presence

Close your eyes for a moment.

Let your body settle.

Inhale slowly through your nose.

Feel your belly rise.

Exhale gently through your mouth.

Feel your body soften.

There is no need to do anything else.

Just this one breath.

And now, another.

Let your attention follow the inhale.

Let it rest with the exhale.

Nothing to fix.

Nothing to change.

Just breathe.

Stay with this rhythm for a few minutes.

Let it remind you that this moment is enough.

listen

March

THE MUDDY ROAD

TWO MONKS WERE TRAVELING during the rainy season.

At the edge of a village, they found a young woman standing before a wide patch of mud, unable to cross in her silk kimono.

Without a word, the older monk lifted her onto his back, carried her across, and set her down. She bowed quickly and vanished into the trees.

The monks continued walking.

Hours passed.

At last, the younger monk burst out, "We're not supposed to touch women. Why did you carry her?"

The older monk looked surprised.

"I set her down hours ago," he said. "Are you still carrying her?"

REFLECTION

Have you ever held onto a judgment longer than the moment that caused it?

____

____

____

____

 Wherever you are, be there totally.

ECKHART TOLLE

EVERY MINUTE IS TEN THOUSAND YEARS

The student asked, "When will I be enlightened?"

The master clapped his hands.

"Ten thousand years have passed," he said.

The student blinked. "But—wasn't that just a moment?"

The master smiled. "Exactly."

Then he walked away, as if nothing had happened.

And everything had.

REFLECTION

What would change if you treated each moment like it mattered completely?

____
____
____
____

ZEN QUOTE

 A flower does not think of competing with the flower next to it. It just blooms.

ZEN SHIN

MINDFUL MOMENTS

Feel the sun on your skin
Like a golden hand, it touches without needing anything back.

THE BROKEN CUP WAS ALREADY BROKEN

A student dropped the master's cup.

It hit the stone floor and shattered—blue porcelain scattered like fallen sky.

"I'm so sorry," the student said, bowing low. "It was my favorite."

The master nodded. "Mine too."

Then he knelt and began sweeping the shards.

"I drank from it every day," he said, "knowing it was already broken."

The broom made a soft whisper as it moved.

REFLECTION

What do you cherish today that you know won't last forever—and can you love it anyway?

____

____

____

____

ZEN QUOTE

" Before enlightenment, chop wood, carry water. After enlightenment, chop wood, carry water.

ZEN PROVERB

MEDITATION: WHAT FEELS OPEN?

Type: Inner Inquiry with Embodied Awareness

Theme: Curiosity, self-awareness

Close your eyes and take a slow breath in.

Feel the air move through your nose, your chest, your belly.

Now ask yourself gently: *What feels open right now?*

Let your awareness scan your body—

not to fix anything, but to notice.

Maybe there's space behind your eyes.

Room in your chest.

A looseness in your shoulders or hands.

Even the smallest bit of openness counts.

It might feel like warmth.

Or lightness.

Or simply less tension than before.

If nothing feels open, that's okay too.

Your presence is enough.

Sit with this quiet noticing for a few minutes.

Let the feeling of openness—wherever it lives—gently expand.

THE MASTER WHO DID NOT SPEAK

The traveler came a long way to meet the master.

He bowed and asked, "Please—give me a teaching."

The master said nothing.

The traveler waited.

Then he asked again. Louder.

Still, no answer.

Anger rose. "Are you deaf? Or just proud?"

The master sat, unmoving.

Finally, the traveler sank to the floor.

His words ran out before his breath did.

In the stillness that followed, he began to hear everything else.

REFLECTION

When was the last time you truly listened—without needing to reply?

ZEN QUOTE

> To understand everything is to forgive everything.

BUDDHA

THE FOX MONK

Long ago, a monk was asked, "Does a person who practices Zen still fall under the law of cause and effect?"

"No," he answered.

And for that answer, he was reborn five hundred times—as a fox.

One evening, he appeared outside a temple, his eyes gold in the dusk.

He told his story to the current master. "Can you free me?" he asked.

The master replied, "Do not ignore cause and effect."

The fox bowed.

"I understand now," he said. Then he vanished.

The next day, they found the body of an old fox beneath the rocks.

The monks held a funeral for him.

REFLECTION

What are the subtle consequences of denying responsibility for your actions?

____

____

____

____

ZEN QUOTE

 The quieter you become, the more you can hear.

RAM DASS

ONE HAND CLAPPING

A student asked, "What is the sound of one hand clapping?"

The master paused.

A breeze passed through the open window, stirring the corner of a scroll.

A bird called out, then went silent.

The student waited for an answer.

Eventually, he forgot he was waiting.

REFLECTION

Are you waiting for an answer that may only come when you stop looking for it?

____

____

____

____

ZEN QUOTE

No snowflake ever falls in the wrong place.

ZEN PROVERB

MINDFUL MOMENTS

Drink your tea with both hands
Hold it like something precious. Let it warm more than just your fingers.

begin

THE MASTER'S ROBE

On his final day, the master folded his robe and placed it on a stone.

"Let the one who understands Zen take this," he said.

His disciples bowed their heads.

One stepped forward, then paused. Another opened his mouth, then closed it.

One by one, they turned and walked away.

The robe stayed on the stone.

The wind lifted a corner, then let it fall.

REFLECTION

What truth in your life feels too simple to claim—and too heavy to carry?

____

____

____

____

ZEN QUOTE

Barn's burnt down — now I can see the moon.

MIZUTA MASAHIDE

MEDITATION: THE LEAF IN THE WIND

Type: Visualization

Theme: Letting go, trust

Imagine a single leaf drifting through the air.

The wind carries it this way, then that—

without effort, without resistance.

Now, close your eyes.

Take a deep breath.

Begin to notice your thoughts, one by one.

No need to hold them.

Just watch as they appear.

Each thought is like a leaf—rising, drifting, falling.

Let them come and go.

Let them turn and spin and fade.

You don't need to follow them.

You don't need to stop them.

Just breathe and notice.

The wind knows where to take them.

Stay with this image for a few minutes.

Let your thoughts move like leaves—softly, freely, without effort.

exhale

THE MOON IN THE WATER

The thief crept in at midnight, expecting coins or gold.

He found only an old man, sitting by the window, watching the sky.

"I have nothing worth stealing," the master said. "But please—take these." He handed the thief his robe and his blanket.

Embarrassed, the thief took them and hurried into the dark.

The master returned to the window.

He looked up at the moon, round and clear.

"I wish I could give him this," he whispered.

The moonlight spilled through the open window, touching everything.

REFLECTION

____

____

____

ZEN QUOTE

If you light a lamp for someone else, it will also brighten your path.

BUDDHA

April

notice

THE EMPTY TEACUP

A PROFESSOR CAME to the Zen master, eager to learn.

He spoke at length about his studies—his readings, his theories, his insights into the nature of things.

The master nodded politely and began to pour tea.

The cup filled. Then it overflowed. The professor watched as it spilled onto the table, then the floor.

"Stop!" he said. "It's already full."

The master set the teapot down.

"And so is your mind," he said.

REFLECTION

What are you too full of right now to receive something new?

____

____

____

____

ZEN QUOTE

When the mind is still, the beauty of the self is seen.

B.K.S. IYENGAR

Look at the sky
Big. Open. Blue. A place where thoughts go to rest.

IS THAT SO?

A young woman became pregnant, and when pressed, she claimed the father was the village Zen master.

Her parents were outraged. They confronted him, scolding and shaming.

He listened calmly and said, "Is that so?"

When the baby was born, they brought it to him. "You must care for your child," they demanded.

He took the baby in his arms. "Is that so?" he said again.

He raised the child with tenderness.

A year later, the mother confessed. The real father was a boy from the market.

The family came back in tears, apologized, and reclaimed the child.

The master handed the baby over.

"Is that so?" he said.

REFLECTION

What might change if you let go of needing to be right in every situation?

____

____

____

____

ZEN QUOTE

> He who knows others is wise; he who knows himself is enlightened.

LAO TZU

MEDITATION: YOUR QUIET CENTER

Type: Breath Anchor with Visualization

Theme: Grounding, stability

Take a slow breath in.

And another out.

Now imagine a still pond deep inside you.

Even if the surface ripples with thoughts or feelings, the water below stays calm.

This is your quiet center—

a peaceful place inside that doesn't get swept away.

With every breath, feel yourself settling into this peace.

The pond is not far away—it's just beneath the noise.

Let the world move around you.

Let this place stay still.

Breathe here for a few minutes.

Let your quiet center hold you steady.

FINGER POINTING AT THE MOON

One night, the teacher and student walked beneath the stars.

The teacher stopped and pointed. "Look," he said. "The moon."

The student stared at the teacher's finger. "It's long," he said. "And graceful. Your nails are clean."

The teacher said nothing.

Above them, the moon hung perfectly still in the sky.

REFLECTION

What are you focusing on right now—the finger, or what it's pointing to?

____
____
____
____

 Nothing ever goes away until it has taught us what we need to know.

PEMA CHÖDRÖN

SWEEP THE GARDEN

"Sweep the garden," the master said.

The monk swept.

"Again," said the master.

The monk swept again—gathering even the hidden leaves beneath the stones.

"Again."

He began to notice the wind.

The way the rake sang over the gravel.

The space between one leaf falling and another landing.

After the fourth time, the master stepped outside, looked around, and nodded.

"Now," he said, "it is as it is."

REFLECTION

What task in your life could become practice—if you stopped rushing to finish it?

____

____

____

____

ZEN QUOTE

Drink your tea slowly and reverently, as if it is the axis on which the world earth revolves.

THÍCH NHẤT HẠNH

MINDFUL MOMENTS

Close your eyes for one minute
Not to block the world—but to see what's inside.

NOTHING EXISTS

"Master," the student asked, "does anything truly exist?"

"No," said the master.

The next day, the student returned. "Then… does nothing exist?"

"Yes," said the master.

On the third day: "So both exist and do not exist?"

The master shrugged. "If you say so."

"And if I don't?"

"Then not."

The student opened his mouth.

Then closed it.

Then went out to sweep the garden.

REFLECTION

How much of what you believe is just a reflection of the words you use?

ZEN QUOTE

 Awareness is the greatest agent for change.

ECKHART TOLLE

MEDITATION: WHAT IS GENTLE TODAY?

Type: Inner Inquiry with Embodiment

Theme: Kindness, softness

Sit quietly and take a soft, steady breath.

Let your shoulders drop.

Let your hands rest gently where they are.

Now ask yourself: *What feels gentle today?*

Not in your mind—but in your body.

Notice the breath as it moves in and out.

Notice how your chest rises and settles.

Feel the warmth in your hands, or the quiet space around you.

Let your body show you where gentleness lives.

Not everything has to be strong.

There is power in soft things too.

Stay with this softness for a few minutes.

Be gentle, quiet, and still.

THE DOG WITH BUDDHA-NATURE

A monk asked, "Does a dog have Buddha-nature?"

The master replied, "Mu."

Nothing more.

The monk bowed.

The question never left him.

pause

REFLECTION

Could "Mu" be your invitation to sit, not solve?

ZEN QUOTE

The wave does not need to die to become water. It is already water.

THÍCH NHẤT HẠNH

THE MIRROR THAT DOESN'T REFLECT

A disciple found an old mirror in the monastery's attic.

No matter how he polished it, it showed nothing back—no face, no light, not even shadow.

He brought it to the master.

"This mirror is broken," he said.

The master held it, turned it once, and said, "Perhaps it's not the mirror that's missing."

The disciple leaned closer, searching.

The glass remained still. So did the master.

REFLECTION

____

____

____

____

ZEN QUOTE

> You should sit in meditation for 20 minutes a day — unless you're too busy. Then you should sit for an hour.

ZEN PROVERB

May

THE SMILING CORPSE

BEFORE HE DIED, the old master gave a final instruction:

"When I go, don't weep. Laugh. Death is not a tragedy—it's the punchline."

But when the day came, his students gathered around the pyre in solemn silence.

They lit the fire. They chanted. Not one smiled.

Then— a loud *pop* from inside the flames. The pyre cracked, and something burst with a great hiss.

The students jumped. Then someone remembered: The master had hidden fireworks in his robes.

Sparks flew upward into the sky, bright as astonishment.

Laughter followed, and did not stop for a long, long time.

REFLECTION

How do you want to be remembered—by the silence you leave, or the laughter?

____

____

____

____

ZEN QUOTE

 If your mind isn't clouded by unnecessary things, this is the best season of your life.

WU-MEN

MINDFUL MOMENTS

Trace a leaf with your finger
Every line is a secret path. Nature's handwriting, just for you.

THE PRICE OF A GOOSE EGG

A wealthy merchant visited the monastery.

"I seek enlightenment," he said, "and I'm willing to pay generously."

The master nodded, disappeared into the back room, and returned holding a goose egg.

He placed it in the merchant's hands.

"This is it," he said.

The merchant frowned. "What does this mean?"

The master smiled. "You asked for value. I gave you breakfast."

The merchant looked at the egg, then at the sky.

He walked away very slowly.

He did not drop it.

REFLECTION

Have you ever missed a gift because you expected something more dramatic?

____

____

____

____

ZEN QUOTE

Those who seek the easy way do not seek the true way.

DŌGEN ZENJI

MEDITATION: THE BELL WITHIN

Type: Visualization

Theme: Stillness, clarity

Imagine a bell resting deep inside you.

Silent. Steady.

It doesn't ring unless you invite it.

Now take a breath.

As you exhale, imagine gently striking that inner bell.

Feel the sound expand through your chest, your belly, your whole body.

You don't need to hear it—just feel it.

A quiet vibration that softens everything.

Each breath is another soft chime.

Each breath carries calm.

Sit with this feeling for a few minutes.

Let your breath be the bell that calms you.

CARRYING THE RAFT

A student built a raft to cross a wide river. It carried him safely to the other side.

Grateful, he hoisted it onto his back and continued his journey.

By the second day, he was sweating. By the third, stumbling. By the fourth, he collapsed.

The master found him lying in the dust, raft still strapped to his shoulders.

"Why are you still carrying it?" the master asked.

"It saved me," the student said.

The master nodded. "And now it weighs you down."

REFLECTION

What once helped you—but now holds you back?

____

____

____

____

ZEN QUOTE

 A wise man, recognizing that the world is but an illusion, does not act as if it is real, so he escapes the suffering.

BUDDHA

NO COLD, NO HEAT

On a winter morning, a monk muttered, "Too cold."

In summer, he sighed, "Too hot."

One day, he asked the master, "How do we escape this suffering of heat and cold?"

The master replied, "Go where there's no hot or cold."

"But where is that?"

The master said, "When it's cold—shiver. When it's hot—sweat."

REFLECTION

What discomfort are you trying to escape—when simply feeling it might be the way through?

____

____

____

____

ZEN QUOTE

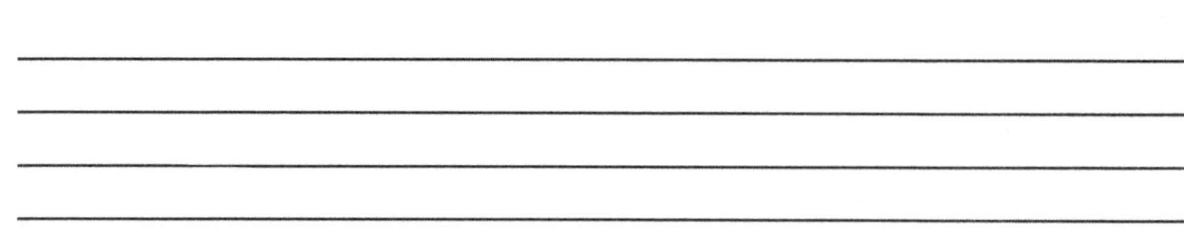

What was never lost can never be found.

ZEN SAYING

THE SOUND OF RAIN

Late one night, a monk sat beside the master as rain tapped gently on the temple roof.

He whispered, "What does enlightenment sound like?"

The master closed his eyes.

Outside, water slid from leaves, dripped from eaves, pooled in the stone basin.

After a long silence, the master said, "It sounds like this."

The monk listened.

He never asked again.

open

REFLECTION

Do you need words to understand something—or can you let the silence do the teaching?

____

____

____

____

ZEN QUOTE

The ten thousand things return to the one. Where does the one return to?

ZEN KOAN

MINDFUL MOMENTS

Smile at someone, even yourself
It's a tiny sunrise. No one has to see it to feel it.

THE MASTER'S FOOTSTEPS

The student followed the master everywhere.

He copied his gait, his way of bowing, even the way he sipped his tea.

Each day, the master walked the garden path barefoot. The student followed, placing his feet in the same prints.

One morning, the student rose early to prepare—and found no footprints.

The master was gone.

He stood for a long while, staring at the untouched earth.

Then, for the first time, he took a step of his own.

REFLECTION

Who are you following so closely that you've forgotten your own path?

____

____

____

____

ZEN QUOTE

Don't seek the truth. Just drop your opinions.

ZEN MASTER SENG-TS'AN

KAI TSUKIMI

settle

MEDITATION: BREATHING WITH THE EARTH

Type: Breath Anchor with Visualization

Theme: Grounding, connection

Sit comfortably and feel the ground beneath you.

With each inhale, imagine drawing strength from the earth.

With each exhale, let your weight sink down gently.

You are connected and rooted like a tree.

Supported, steady, safe.

Feel the breath rise through you like the energy in a trunk.

Feel it soften and return to the ground.

Let your body breathe with the earth.

Stay with this rhythm for a few minutes.

Let the ground hold you steady.

THE FLOATING LANTERN

A monk lit a lantern and set it gently on the river.

It drifted downstream, casting trembling light on the dark water.

"Is the lantern moving?" he asked the master. "Or the water?" "Or me?"

The master watched the lantern float out of sight.

Then said, "Yes."

REFLECTION

____

____

____

____

ZEN QUOTE

To live in the present moment is a miracle.

THÍCH NHẤT HẠNH

THE MASTER WHO INSULTED HIM

The student approached the master with reverence and a carefully prepared question.

Before he could speak, the master looked him over and said,

"Too slow. Too proud. Too full of books."

The student's mouth fell open.

"I only came to learn," he muttered.

The master turned away. "Then learn."

That night, the student couldn't sleep.

He replayed the insult again and again—like a koan carved into his chest.

At dawn, he returned to the garden.

The master was sweeping fallen leaves.

The student bowed. "Why did you insult me yesterday?"

The master paused, then flicked a leaf toward him with the broom.

"You've carried those words all night," he said. "Why didn't you leave them with me?"

The wind took the rest of the leaves.

And the student said nothing.

REFLECTION

What if being insulted was the lesson—not the mistake?

____

____

____

____

ZEN QUOTE

 When the mind clings to nothing, even the wind stops.

ZEN SAYING

MINDFUL MOMENTS

Wash your hands with full attention
Water, soap, skin. Each swirl a small ceremony.

THE CUP THAT FILLED ITSELF

A novice sat alone in the meditation hall, his mind as empty as the teacup before him.

He had fasted for three days, hoping for a sign.

The master entered without a word and placed a kettle on the low table.

"Tea?" he asked.

The novice nodded. The master poured.

But though no tea flowed, the cup began to fill.

Steam curled. Fragrance bloomed. The cup overflowed with nothing at all.

The novice stared, then blinked.

"Is this... a trick?"

The master sipped from his own empty cup. "Only if you're thirsty for answers."

The novice laughed, though he wasn't sure why.

The cup shimmered, then was still.

From that day on, he never again asked to be filled.

And yet—he always was.

allow

Can you laugh at the unexplainable... and feel complete anyway?

ZEN QUOTE

Even death is not to be feared by one who has lived wisely.

BUDDHA

MEDITATION: THE GOLDEN THREAD

Type: Visualization with Body Awareness

Theme: Connection, wholeness

Close your eyes and imagine a golden thread inside your body.

It begins at the top of your head and runs gently down through your throat,

your chest, your belly, your legs—all the way to your feet.

This thread connects every part of you.

Linking you together with warmth and light.

As you breathe, imagine that golden thread glowing softly.

You are whole.

You are here.

Rest with this image for a few minutes.

Let yourself feel connected from within.

June

THE MAN WHO FORGOT HIS NAME

IN A FOREST HERMITAGE, a man sat cross-legged beneath a pine for so long that birds forgot to fear him.

One day, a passing monk asked, "What is your name?"

The man blinked. His lips moved, but no sound came. He searched the folds of memory, like rummaging through old robes—but nothing. No name, no story, no one to be embarrassed.

He began to laugh.

The monk looked puzzled.

"I have no name," said the man, "and no problem."

He watched the wind rearrange the grass. Leaves whispered secrets he no longer needed to understand.

When he rose, he bowed to the sun, to the ants, to the stranger before him.

"Then who are you?" asked the monk.

The man smiled. "Exactly."

REFLECTION

Who are you when you're not performing for anyone—including yourself?

> The moon does not fight. It attacks no one. It does not worry. It does not try to crush others. It keeps to its course.

DENG MING-DAO

THE SOUND BENEATH THE SOUND

Each morning, the great bronze bell called the monks to zazen.

One student winced with every strike. "Master," he said, "the bell is too loud. It rattles my thoughts."

The master nodded and said nothing.

The next morning, the bell rang again—deep, resounding, immovable.

The student covered his ears.

The master whispered, "Close your ears if you must, but open your listening."

That night, while the crickets stitched silence into the dark, the student sat alone by the bell.

He listened to its echo long after the ringing stopped. Then he listened deeper still.

There—between the silence and the echo—he heard it.

A sound not made of sound.

REFLECTION

Have you ever heard something deeper than sound itself?

ZEN QUOTE

Walk as if you are kissing the Earth with your feet.

THÍCH NHẤT HẠNH

MINDFUL MOMENTS

Sit without doing

No task. No goal. Just the moment sitting with you.

THE WOODEN BUDDHA

When the temple caught fire, monks rushed to save scriptures, scrolls, bells.

By dawn, it was ash and smoke.

Only the Buddha statue remained—blackened, half-buried in soot. Its head was gone. One hand, melted. Still, it sat in the lotus posture, as if watching the flames rise and fall.

The villagers gathered in silence.

Children placed flowers at its feet. An old woman whispered prayers to the empty air where the face once smiled.

A novice asked, "Should we carve a new one?"

The abbot shook his head. "This one has seen fire. Let it teach."

From then on, they bowed not to its shape, but to its stillness.

REFLECTION

What stories do your scars now teach?

ZEN QUOTE

Flow with whatever may happen, and let your mind be free. Stay centered by accepting whatever you are doing. This is the ultimate.

ZHUANGZI

unfold

MEDITATION: THE WARM STONE

Type: Visualization with Sensory Grounding

Theme: Safety, calm

Imagine a smooth stone warmed by the sun.

You pick it up and place it in your palm.

Feel its warmth sinking into your hand,

spreading through your wrist, up your arm, into your chest.

Each breath you take helps the warmth grow.

It moves through your body like sunlight under the skin.

Let the stone melt any tension.

Let it soften the stress.

Stay with the warmth for a few minutes.

Let it remind you—you are safe.

THE MASTER'S WHISPER

The master was dying.

Students gathered around, eyes shining with urgency. Some clutched notebooks. One wept quietly into his robe.

The youngest leaned in and said, "Please, Master—your final teaching."

The old man's breath rattled like wind through dry reeds.

He beckoned the student closer. Lips barely moving, he whispered a single sentence into the boy's ear.

Then he was gone.

The student's face went pale.

"What did he say?" the others asked.

But the student only shook his head—once, slowly.

He never spoke of it.

Years passed. He became a teacher himself, but when asked the secret of his wisdom, he would only smile, as if remembering something too vast for words.

Or perhaps nothing at all.

REFLECTION

Can something be sacred even if it's never shared?

____

____

____

____

ZEN QUOTE

A man is not called wise because he talks and talks again; but if he is peaceful, loving and fearless then he is in truth called wise.

BUDDHA

THE CLOUD THAT FORGOT TO RAIN

The monk sat day and night, memorizing sutras, polishing thoughts, arranging wisdom like stones in a perfect circle.

Still, his heart felt heavy.

"I can't let go," he confessed to the master. "My mind won't stop."

The master looked up at the sky, where a lone cloud hovered—gray, swollen, unmoving.

"Even clouds," he said, "must let go if they wish to drift."

The monk looked again.

By dusk, the cloud had vanished. Not with thunder. Not with drama.

Just a few drops in the moss. A little more space in the sky.

That night, the monk stopped studying.

He listened to the quiet.

And let it rain.

REFLECTION

Can you let your thoughts drift without trying to manage them?

____

____

____

____

ZEN QUOTE

 In the stillness of the mind, I saw myself as I am —
unbound.

NISARGADATTA MAHARAJ

MINDFUL MOMENTS

Listen until the sound fades
Not just the sound—what comes after it.

A CUP OF COOL WATER

Dust covered the pilgrim's robes. His sandals were torn. He had crossed deserts, climbed mountains, left behind all he knew.

At last, he arrived at the hermitage.

The master said nothing, only vanished inside and returned with a single cup—simple, ceramic, chipped at the rim.

The pilgrim drank.

Not hurriedly, not with desperation. Just one sip… then another.

When the cup was empty, he set it down.

"I thought there would be more," he said.

The master nodded. "There is. But not in the cup."

The wind moved through the trees like breath through lungs.

And the pilgrim realized: he was no longer thirsty.

remember

When have you received less than you expected—but still felt whole?

____

____

____

____

ZEN QUOTE

When thoughts arise, then do all things arise. When thoughts vanish, then do all things vanish.

HUANG PO

MEDITATION: BREATHING LIKE THE OCEAN

Type: Breath Anchor with Visualization

Theme: Rhythm, flow

Breathe in…

breathe out…

Now imagine the ocean.

Waves rolling in, waves rolling out.

Your breath follows the same rhythm.

Inhale, like a wave gathering at sea.

Exhale, like it returning to shore.

Let your breath be tidal.

Natural. Endless. Soft.

Feel the rise in your belly, the release in your shoulders.

Breathe like the ocean for a few minutes.

Let yourself move with its rhythm.

THE HIDDEN STONE

Each morning, the child found the same smooth stone beneath the banyan tree.

She carried it in her pocket, skipped it across ponds, gave it names like "Moon Seed" and "Turtle Egg."

It made no sound. It asked for nothing. It simply was.

One day, the stone was gone.

She searched the roots, the reeds, her coat—nothing.

She sat where it used to rest and cried.

Later, an old traveler passed by. She told him her sorrow.

He looked at her palms. "You held a diamond," he said softly.

"A diamond?" she gasped. "Why didn't anyone tell me?"

He smiled. "You loved it well. What more would you have done?"

Have you ever cherished something deeply without realizing how rare it was?

ZEN QUOTE

Peace comes from within. Do not seek it without.

BUDDHA

THE TEMPLE WITHOUT DOORS

The villagers watched with curiosity as the master's temple took shape —elegant stone, curved roof, polished floors.

But no doors.

They waited. Still none.

At last, someone asked, "How will we enter?"

The master ran his hand along the smooth wall and said, "Those who need to enter will find a way in."

Some laughed. Others frowned. Most wandered off.

But one morning, a child was found sitting inside, legs crossed, smiling.

"How did you get in?" they asked.

She shrugged. "I stopped looking for the door."

From that day on, the temple was always open—and still without doors.

REFLECTION

Have you ever found your way not by pushing—but by pausing?

____

____

____

____

ZEN QUOTE

There is no need to seek truth, only to stop cherishing opinions.

JIANZHI SENGCAN

MINDFUL MOMENTS

Stretch your arms with care
Like you're waking up from a long, kind dream.

July

THE BAMBOO CAGE

THE MONK FOUND the bird shivering in the rain and brought it inside.

He wove a bamboo cage with care, set it by the window, and gave the bird seeds and songs. "Here," he said, "you are safe."

Each morning, the bird sang. And the monk smiled, believing the song meant gratitude.

But over time, the notes thinned. Then stopped.

One morning, the monk sat beside the cage. He waited. Silence.

He opened the door.

The bird did not fly out. Not right away. But it looked at him—once—then vanished into the trees.

That evening, the wind moved through the empty cage like breath through old prayer beads.

And the monk understood something he had not meant to do.

REFLECTION

When have you confused care with control?

____

____

____

____

 The great way is not difficult if you just don't pick and choose.

SENGCAN

MEDITATION: THE GARDEN INSIDE

Type: Visualization with Body Awareness

Theme: Growth, nourishment

Close your eyes and imagine a garden inside your chest.

There is soft earth, warm light, and space for things to grow.

With each inhale, imagine sunlight touching the soil.

With each exhale, roots stretch a little deeper.

Maybe there's a seed in this garden—something you're nurturing.

A feeling. A dream. A part of yourself.

You don't need to name it. Just feel it there.

Let your breath nourish the garden.

Let the stillness help it grow.

Sit with this image for a few minutes.

Feel the quiet beauty of what you're tending.

INK ON WATER

All night, the student wrote.

Draft after draft, until at last—seven strokes, a breath of silence, one final mark.

He bowed to the parchment.

But as he rose, a breeze lifted the page from his desk. It floated, spun gently… and landed in the pond outside.

He ran to it, watching the ink bloom and vanish in ripples.

Gone.

Trembling, he brought his empty hands to the master.

The old man looked at the water, now still, and said, "Ah… now it is complete."

The student blinked. "But it's lost."

"Only the paper," said the master. "Not the poem."

REFLECTION

What if completion isn't in the keeping, but in the letting go?

____

____

____

____

 Zen is the unsymbolization of the world.

REGINALD HORACE BLYTH

THE STRANGER'S SMILE

Each evening at dusk, a man appeared at the monastery gates.

He never spoke.

He only bowed, smiled at the gatekeeper, and turned back down the hill.

At first, the gatekeeper thought little of it.

But the man came again the next night. And the next. Seasons passed. Then years.

They never exchanged a word.

One day, the man did not come.

Nor the next.

The gatekeeper waited longer than usual. Finally, he closed the gate.

That night, he sat by the lantern and wept—though he could not say why.

Just a smile, after all.

Just a stranger.

And yet.

trust

REFLECTION

Can a connection exist without words—or even without knowing someone's name?

ZEN QUOTE

One moment can change a day, one day can change a life, and one life can change the world.

BUDDHA

THE MASTER WHO FORGOT HE WAS A MASTER

He swept the road each morning. Tended the temple garden. Fed the crows by hand.

To the villagers, he was just Old Karo—the one who hummed to rocks and bowed to puddles.

One day, a traveler gasped at the sight of him.

"You're Master Karo! The Sage of the Three Mountains!"

The old man scratched his head. "Am I?"

"Yes! You vanished years ago—legends say you attained complete freedom!"

The old man looked at his broom. "I wondered why sweeping felt so light."

Then he bowed, not as a master, but as a man with dirt on his robes and nothing to prove.

REFLECTION

What would change if you let go of your titles, roles, or reputation?

____

____

____

____

ZEN QUOTE

If you want to travel the Way, don't reproach the world. Accept everything and take the Way as it is.

RINZAI

MINDFUL MOMENTS

Notice the texture of your clothes
Soft or rough, warm or cool—it's always touching you back.

slow

RAIN IN THE TEACUP

The master left his favorite teacup on the porch—fine porcelain, hairline cracks like rivers through clay.

A sudden rain came.

The novice rushed out, heart pounding. Too late. The cup was half-full of sky.

He brought it in, bowing low. "Forgive me, Master. I should have—"

The master took the cup, held it to the light, and drank.

He smacked his lips. "It tastes like sky."

The novice blinked.

The master set the cup down and smiled. "Perhaps it always did. Today, I remembered to notice."

REFLECTION

What beauty or truth has shown up in your life by accident—
when you weren't trying?

MEDITATION: THE SHELL OF YOUR BODY

Type: Breath and Body Anchor

Theme: Protection, awareness

Bring your attention to the edges of your body.

The skin that wraps around you.

The surface that meets the world.

Breathe in, and feel the space within.

Breathe out, and feel the gentle boundary that holds you.

From your toes to your scalp, this body is your shelter.

Strong and alive.

Notice the quiet inside this shell.

The calm it offers.

Rest here for a few minutes.

Let your body be your home.

THE SHADOW OF THE BELL

"Tomorrow," the master said, "rise before dawn and listen for the bell."

The disciple did as told. He sat in the courtyard, wrapped in mist and silence.

No bell rang.

No sound at all—only the hush of trees and the faint pulse of his own breath.

At sunrise, he approached the master.

"Did the bell not ring?"

The master looked up from his tea. "It did."

"I heard nothing."

"Then listen again," the master said, "to what remains after the ringing stops."

The disciple returned to the courtyard.

And waited for what was no longer there.

REFLECTION

What have you been waiting to hear... that may have already spoken?

____

____

____

____

ZEN QUOTE

Meditation is not to escape from society, but to come back to ourselves and see what is going on.

THÍCH NHẤT HẠNH

THE APPLE LEFT UNFINISHED

A young monk was given an apple with his morning rice.

He bit once, then saw the abbot approaching and quickly set it aside.

"Discipline," he thought, "is not indulging in pleasure."

The apple sat on his windowsill all day.

By sunset, it had browned. By morning, it drew flies.

Still, he did not touch it.

On the third day, the abbot paused outside his cell and pointed.

"Why haven't you finished your apple?"

"I didn't want to be greedy," the monk replied.

The abbot chuckled and walked on, saying only:

"Waste is a form of greed too."

That night, the monk dreamed of apples raining from the sky—each one rotting before it reached his hands.

When he woke, he ate the apple.

Though soft and sour, it was the sweetest thing he had ever tasted.

REFLECTION

Have you ever denied yourself something good—not out of wisdom, but fear of indulgence?

____

____

____

____

ZEN QUOTE

 He who conquers himself is the mightiest warrior.

CONFUCIUS

MINDFUL MOMENTS

Follow the movement of your breath
In, out. Like waves brushing the shore of your ribs.

THE MASTER'S LAST BOWL

After the master's final breath, the disciples gathered his few belongings.

One remained: a cracked clay bowl, worn smooth by years of tea and silence.

They argued what to do.

"Mend it," said one. "He would want it whole."

"No," said another. "Let it be buried with him."

A third suggested placing it on the altar—honored, untouched.

That night, as moonlight spilled across the floor, the bowl vanished.

In its place: a single cherry blossom, freshly fallen, its petals curled inward like a whispered secret.

No one spoke of the bowl again.

But each brewed tea a little more gently.

REFLECTION

How gently would you move through life if you treated every moment like the master's last bowl?

____

____

____

____

MEDITATION: THE WINDOW OF THE HEART

Type: Inner Inquiry with Visualization

Theme: Openness, compassion

Imagine your heart has a window.

For a moment, let it open just a little.

Feel the breeze come in.

Feel warmth move out.

You don't need to force it open wide.

Even a small crack lets in light.

Breathe gently.

Notice what flows through.

It might be kindness, gratitude, or even a little sadness.

Whatever comes, let it be welcome.

Sit here for a few minutes.

Let your heart stay just as open as it wants to be.

August

THE CUSHION SHARED

IT WAS a cold morning in the meditation hall.

The fire had gone out, and the monks sat like frost-covered statues.

One young monk arrived late. Finding no cushion left, he stood uncertainly by the door.

An elder noticed, lifted his own cushion, and tore it cleanly in two.

He offered half without a word.

The young monk hesitated. "Won't you be uncomfortable?"

The elder smiled. "Only half as much."

They sat, side by side, barely balanced—but still.

Years later, that same young monk, now old himself, saw a student shivering outside the hall.

Without thinking, he tore his cushion in half.

The thread was frayed. The fabric thin.

Still, it held.

REFLECTION

Who in your life needs half a cushion—and would you offer it
without hesitation?

____

____

____

____

> Nothing is more precious than being in the present moment. Fully alive, fully aware.

THÍCH NHẤT HẠNH

THE SAND GARDEN

Each morning, before the sun rose over the temple roof, the master raked the sand.

Lines curved like water, stones placed like pauses in a poem. Not a leaf out of place.

One day, a child wandered in—barefoot, laughing—and danced across the garden, leaving a trail of joy and prints.

The students gasped.

The master looked at the footprints, then at the wind brushing through the pine.

He set down his rake.

"It needed that," he said.

The students never touched the prints.

By the next morning, they were gone.

But the garden seemed more alive than ever.

release

What are you trying so hard to keep perfect that you've forgotten to let life walk through it?

____

____

____

____

ZEN QUOTE

Let your mind be as a floating cloud. Let your body be as the rising sun.

ZEN SAYING

MINDFUL MOMENTS

Watch a candle flicker
A quiet dance that never asks for applause.

THE LANTERN THAT WOULDN'T LIGHT

The student wandered the forest path, clutching a lantern with no flame.

He struck flint, whispered prayers, shook it gently. Still, darkness.

Frustrated, he returned to the temple, moonlight trailing behind him.

"I couldn't find the way," he said. "The lantern won't light."

The master looked up from his tea. "Yet you returned."

"I stumbled. I got lost. I was afraid."

The master smiled. "Even the moon casts enough light to lose your way."

The student blinked.

That night, he left the lantern behind—and walked by moonlight alone.

Not seeing more.

But fearing less.

REFLECTION

Have you ever found your way—not because you could see, but because you kept going?

____

____

____

____

ZEN QUOTE

No thought, no reflection, no analysis, no cultivation, no intention; let it settle itself.

TILOPA

KAI TSUKIMI

MEDITATION: THE MOUNTAIN BENEATH YOU

Type: Visualization with Body Grounding

Theme: Stability, strength

Sit down and feel the weight of your body.

Now imagine you're sitting on a big, steady mountain.

Breathe in.

Feel the mountain rise beneath you.

Breathe out.

Let your weight settle at the top.

No matter what happens around you—winds, noise, distractions—the mountain remains.

And so do you.

You don't have to do anything.

Just sit and be.

Rest here for a few minutes.

Let the mountain hold you steady.

THE MASTER'S COUGH

Every evening, the hall filled with stillness.

Dozens of students, eyes half-closed, breaths softened into the hush of pine needles and dusk.

And then—always—*one cough.*

Short. Dry. The master's.

No one spoke of it. Yet all waited for it, like the temple bell that never needed to ring.

Years passed this way.

Then one evening, the master did not arrive.

The cushions were arranged. The incense lit.

The silence deepened.

And still they sat—listening for the cough that never came.

Some say they still hear it, faint and far, like the echo of a bell long struck.

REFLECTION

Can you sit with what's no longer there—and still feel its presence?

____

____

____

____

ZEN QUOTE

There is no fear for one whose mind is not filled with desires.

BUDDHA

THE DOOR THAT OPENS BOTH WAYS

Two students stood by the temple gate, arguing.

"One must enter to awaken," said the first. "The teachings are inside."

"No," said the second. "One must leave. Awakening is beyond walls."

Their voices rose, sharp as sparrows.

The master arrived, carrying a basket of turnips.

He listened. Then, without a word, he walked through the gate—into the temple.

Moments later, he turned around and walked back out.

He set the basket down between them and said, "The door doesn't care which way you walk."

Then he picked up a turnip and kept walking.

Neither student moved.

But the breeze did.

REFLECTION

What if awakening isn't about where you go—but how you walk?

____

____

____

____

ZEN QUOTE

 The obstacle is the path.

ZEN PROVERB

MINDFUL MOMENTS

Feel your heartbeat
Steady. Strong. A drum you didn't know you were playing.

THREE POUNDS OF FLAX

"What is Buddha?" the monk asked.

Tozan didn't look up.

He was tying a bundle of flax—coarse, golden threads piled like sun-warmed straw in his lap.

He pulled the string tight and said, "Three pounds."

The monk blinked, unsure if he'd heard right.

Tozan blew the dust from his hands, stood up, and carried the flax to the weaving shed.

The monk remained, holding the question like a flame cupped in both palms.

Later that evening, a breeze passed through the empty hall.

And smelled faintly—

of rope,

of sunlight,

of something already answered.

REFLECTION

Have you ever received an answer that didn't make sense—but still felt true?

____
____
____
____

ZEN QUOTE

 Don't try to steer the river.

DEEPAK CHOPRA

MEDITATION: A QUIET GLOW

Type: Breath with Visualization

Theme: Calm, warmth

Close your eyes and imagine a soft glow in your chest.

It could be the size of a candle flame.

Or a little larger, like a sunset.

With each breath in, the glow brightens.

With each breath out, it spreads across your body.

Let it move through your arms, your belly, your back.

There's no rush to go anywhere.

Only light, moving through you with every breath.

Breathe with the glow for a few minutes.

Let it fill you with warmth and calm.

THE BRUSH THAT DREW NOTHING

Each morning, the master sat before a blank scroll, dipped his brush in invisible ink, and began to paint.

The students watched in silence.

"What do you see?" he asked one day.

"Nothing," a novice whispered.

"Good," said the master. "Now you're not distracted."

Another asked, "But what are you painting?"

He smiled. "That depends who's looking."

Years passed. The scrolls filled a shelf, soft and empty.

When the master died, the students unrolled them one by one.

Some wept. Some laughed. Some said they saw mountains.

No one agreed on what wasn't there.

What do you see when there's nothing to distract you?

____

____

____

____

ZEN QUOTE

At the still point of the turning world… there the dance is.

T.S. ELIOT

THE ROOM WITHOUT WALLS

The new student arrived eager, head full of sutras and spine straight with discipline.

The master led him to a clearing in the woods—no roof, no walls, only sky and grass and a single cushion.

"This is your cell," said the master. "Begin your confinement."

The student looked around, puzzled. "But… there's nothing here."

"Exactly."

"But how will I know when I've left?"

The master smiled. "Most never do."

Then he walked away, leaving only silence, wind, and the sound of a bird that refused to stay caged.

REFLECTION

Are you truly free—or just confined by different walls?

ZEN QUOTE

The real meditation is how you live your life.

JON KABAT-ZINN

                                    KAI TSUKIMI

September

THE MONK'S SHADOW

AT SUNSET, the young monk ran circles in the courtyard, twisting and lunging at the long shape on the ground.

"It's trying to escape," he shouted, laughing and breathless. "I almost caught it!"

The master stood at the edge of the light, watching.

Without a word, he stepped forward—placing himself between the boy and the sun.

The shadow vanished.

The monk froze.

"Where did it go?" he whispered.

The master said nothing, only stepped aside again.

And there it was.

The same shape. The same chase.

But something had changed.

The monk bowed—not to the master, but to the light.

REFLECTION

What happens when you stop trying to catch your shadow?

____

____

____

____

 Look past your thoughts so you may drink the pure nectar of This Moment.

RUMI

MINDFUL MOMENTS

Stand barefoot for a moment
No shoes. No rush. Just you and the living floor.

THE TEACUP WITH A CRACK

The student searched the cupboard for the finest cup—smooth glaze, perfect rim.

But only one remained. Old. Cracked. A thin line ran down its side like a healed wound.

Ashamed, he brought it to the master with trembling hands.

"I'm sorry," he said. "It's all I could find."

The master took it without a glance, poured the tea, and drank slowly.

Then he smiled. "It tastes more human this way."

The student looked down at the steaming cup. The crack glistened slightly in the light.

He said nothing. But he no longer looked away.

REFLECTION

Can something be more meaningful because of its flaws—not in spite of them?

____

____

____

____

ZEN QUOTE

To be truly free, you must be willing to stand alone in the truth of who you are.

ADYASHANTI

MEDITATION: WHAT NEEDS YOUR ATTENTION?

Type: Inner Inquiry with Body Awareness

Theme: Listening, compassion

Take a breath and bring your awareness inward.

Ask yourself: *What needs my attention right now?*

Maybe it's a tightness in your shoulders.

A small sadness in your chest.

A flicker of joy in your belly.

Notice how it feels.

Let that part of you feel seen.

Feel heard.

Do not try to change it.

Offer it kindness through your breath.

Sit with this part of you for a few minutes.

Be present with how you're feeling.

THE GATE THAT LED NOWHERE

The traveler crossed deserts, scaled mountains, sat with saints and fools.

All he sought was the gate to enlightenment—golden, hidden, sacred.

One morning, in a field of wind and wild grass, he found it:

A wooden gate. Weathered. Standing alone. No fence, no walls, nothing beyond.

Just the sky.

He walked around it. Touched its frame. Waited for revelation.

Nothing changed.

A child passed by, barefoot, chasing a kite. She ran through the gate and kept running, laughing.

The traveler stood for a long time.

Then he stepped through, paused, and smiled.

The grass felt the same on both sides.

Have you ever searched far and wide, only to discover what you were seeking was never hidden?

ZEN QUOTE

> Don't move. Just die over and over. Don't anticipate. Nothing can save you now because you have only this moment. Not even enlightenment will help you now because there are no other moments. With no future, be true to yourself and express yourself fully. Don't move.

SHUNRYU SUZUKI

THE THREAD OF WIND

As a young monk, he tied a string to a cherry branch.

"To catch the wind," he said.

Each day he checked it—watching the way it danced, hoping to understand what moved it.

Seasons passed. The string faded from red to gray. Frayed. Tangled.

Still, he never took it down.

One evening, much older now, he stood beneath the tree with the master.

The breeze stirred. The string trembled, barely holding on.

The master chuckled. "Still trying to hold breath?"

The monk looked up, then let the wind touch his face, unmeasured.

And the string finally broke.

REFLECTION

What have you been trying to measure, catch, or prove—when it was always meant to move freely?

ZEN QUOTE

Live the actual moment. Only this actual moment is life.

THÍCH NHẤT HẠNH

recieve

THE PILLOW OF STONES

The disciple tossed through the night, his mat too thin, the floor too cruel.

In the morning, he bowed low before the master. "I cannot sleep. The bed is too hard."

The master nodded and returned with a new pillow—beautiful silk, expertly stitched.

The disciple smiled... until he laid his head on it.

It was filled with stones.

He sat up, confused. "Why would you give me this?"

The master said, "Because you still believe comfort comes from what lies beneath you."

That night, too tired to protest, the disciple rested anyway.

And dreamed of rivers flowing over rock.

REFLECTION

Where in your life are you waiting for comfort instead of learning to rest anyway?

____

____

____

____

 Don't be a slave to your thoughts. Instead, be their witness.

AMIT RAY

MINDFUL MOMENTS

Pick up one thing with care
Even a pebble can feel like a treasure when noticed.

THE RIVER THAT WAITED

The novice stood at the edge of the stream, water loud with urgency.

"What if I slip?" he asked.

"Then you will learn to swim," said the master.

But the novice hesitated.

"I'll wait," he said. "Until it's safe."

So he watched the water for days. Then weeks.

One morning, the stream was gone—reduced to a trickle of pebbles and dust.

The novice looked across at the empty bank, unsure what had changed.

The master appeared beside him and whispered, "You missed it."

"Missed what?"

"The current that would've carried you."

REFLECTION

What have you postponed until "the right moment"—and did it pass while you waited?

____

____

____

____

ZEN QUOTE

Don't seek, don't search, don't ask, don't knock, don't demand—relax.

OSHO

MEDITATION: THE SKY ABOVE YOU

Type: Visualization

Theme: Perspective, spaciousness

Close your eyes and imagine the sky above you.

Vast, endless, and open.

Now feel that same spaciousness above your head and shoulders.

Notice the vastness of your imagination.

No matter what thoughts are cluttering your mind, there is always a spaciousness underneath.

You don't need to reach it.

You are already in it.

Like clouds, let your thoughts flow by.

And recognize that the sky will always be there.

Stay with this feeling for a few minutes.

Let the sky remind you of the silence under the noise.

THE ECHO'S ECHO

While meditating in the mountains, the student heard it—a faint voice calling his name.

He rose in awe. "A sign!" he said. "Proof that I am chosen!"

He returned to the temple, breathless. "The mountain spoke to me."

The master raised an eyebrow. "What did it say?"

"My name."

The master leaned close and whispered, "Even illusions echo."

That night, the student returned to the mountain. Sat still.

Listened.

He heard it again—but softer now, unsure of whose voice it had ever been.

And in that not-knowing, something grew quiet inside him.

Have you ever mistaken your own thoughts or hopes for a message from outside?

____

____

____

____

ZEN QUOTE

When you understand one thing through and through, you understand everything. When you try to understand everything, you understand nothing.

SHUNRYU SUZUKI

THE EMPTY BRUSH

For ten years, the artist prepared.

She rose before dawn, arranged her brushes, boiled her ink—and painted nothing.

"Waiting," she would say, "for the right moment."

One morning, she took no ink at all.

She dipped her brush in water, walked to the edge of the garden, and drew a single line in the sand.

By noon, it was gone—wind-smoothed, sun-faded.

A student watching asked, "What was it?"

She smiled. "The painting."

"But where is it?"

She looked at the sky. "Where it always was."

REFLECTION

Can a moment be meaningful even if it leaves no trace?

____

____

____

____

ZEN QUOTE

Rest in natural great peace, this exhausted mind beaten helpless by karma and neurotic thought.

NYOSHUL KHEN RINPOCHE

soften

October

THE THREAD

ONE MORNING, the monk awoke to find a red thread tied gently around his wrist.

He asked the other monks if they had seen who tied it. They hadn't. He asked the master. The master only smiled.

He tugged at the knot. It tightened.

He tugged harder. It bit into the skin.

So he left it.

Days passed. He swept the garden, bowed at dawn, served tea—all with the thread brushing softly against his sleeve, neither loosening nor breaking.

He began to forget it was there.

Then one morning, it was gone.

No mark. No trace.

Only an odd lightness in his hand.

And the faintest sense that something had just let go.

REFLECTION

Could letting go feel less like a decision, and more like something that simply... happens?

____

____

____

____

ZEN QUOTE

No one saves us but ourselves. No one can and no one may. We ourselves must walk the path.

BUDDHA

MINDFUL MOMENTS

Watch a cloud pass
A traveler with no suitcase, no map, no hurry.

THE LAST STEP

After many years and many blisters, the traveler reached the peak.

He had crossed deserts, forded rivers, outlasted storms. His beard had grown white. His staff was worn smooth by his hand.

At the summit, there was no grand view. No sky-splitting revelation.

Only a single stone step.

It led upward—into mist.

He stood before it for a long time.

Then, without sigh or ceremony, he sat down beside it.

He took off his shoes, emptied out the pebbles, and smiled.

"This is far enough," he said.

The mist thickened. The step disappeared.

But the mountain did not.

REFLECTION

What if "enough" isn't a place you reach—but something you realize?

____

____

____

____

ZEN QUOTE

I have no special talents. I am only passionately curious.

ALBERT EINSTEIN

MEDITATION: A SOFT PLACE TO LAND

Type: Breath & Body Grounding

Theme: Safety, rest

Close your eyes and take a deep, gentle breath.

Feel your body making contact with the ground.

Now imagine lying in a quiet meadow—

the earth beneath you is warm, soft, and alive.

The grass feels like a cushion.

The sky stretches endlessly above.

Let yourself sink a little deeper.

There is nothing to hold up.

Nothing to prove.

With each breath, feel the ground supporting you completely.

It asks for nothing in return.

Let your weight fall into it.

Let your breath slow down.

Rest here for a few minutes.

Let yourself be fully relaxed.

THE MASTER'S SHOES

At dawn, the student slipped into the master's shoes.

He walked the temple path slowly, hoping to feel something—clarity, insight, transformation.

But the stones felt the same. So did the wind. So did he.

All day, he wandered in circles.

The shoes were stiff. They pinched at the toes.

The next morning, he returned them quietly to the master's door.

He found the old man barefoot in the garden, his heels dusted with earth.

"I liked the feel of soil," the master said without looking up. "Those shoes were too tight anyway."

He patted the dirt, soft and sure.

stay

REFLECTION

Have you ever tried to walk someone else's path—and found it didn't fit?

____

____

____

____

ZEN QUOTE

The mind is everything. What you think, you become.

BUDDHA

THE EMPTY DRUM

Each morning, before the sun crested the hills, the temple drum called out—deep, steady, waking the valley.

But one morning, there was no sound.

The monks gathered, confused. The drum sat untouched. No mallet. No echo.

They whispered theories. They checked the ropes.

Nothing was broken. Nothing was wrong.

That afternoon, a child from the village climbed the steps and found the master sipping broth beneath the eaves.

"I heard the drum today," the child said.

The master looked up, eyes soft.

"Then it was struck well."

REFLECTION

Can presence make more noise than action?

ZEN QUOTE

> A man is great not because he hasn't failed; a man is great because failure hasn't stopped him.

CONFUCIUS

THE JAR OF STILLNESS

On the altar sat a plain glass jar, filled with water drawn from the temple well.

Each morning, the master stirred it—once, gently.

Ripples lapped the sides. Silt rose, swirled, and slowly settled.

The students watched, never asking why.

Then one morning, the master left it untouched.

Days passed. The water cleared. Stones appeared at the bottom—small, smooth, forgotten.

A student finally asked, "Why don't you stir it anymore?"

The master looked at the jar.

"Now we can see the bottom."

REFLECTION

When do you confuse motion with progress?

____

____

____

____

ZEN QUOTE

A journey of a thousand miles begins with a single step.

LAO TZU

Place your hand on your heart
It's been with you all along. Say thank you.

THE MONK WHO DIDN'T ARRIVE

Word spread that a great monk was coming.

The students swept every corner of the temple. They aired out cushions, trimmed the lantern wicks, arranged fruit just so.

Then they waited.

He did not arrive that day.

Nor the next.

Weeks passed. The fruit withered. The cushions gathered dust.

Still, they waited.

One morning, without announcement, the teacher entered the hall and bowed toward the empty cushion.

"He has taught us enough," she said.

No one spoke.

But a few began to sweep again.

REFLECTION

Who or what have you been preparing for... that might never come?

____

____

____

____

ZEN QUOTE

 You cannot travel the path until you have become the path itself.

BUDDHA

MEDITATION: THE LIGHT YOU CARRY

Type: Visualization with Inner Awareness

Theme: Inner peace, self-worth

Close your eyes and imagine a gentle light inside you.

It's always been there, since the very beginning.

This light doesn't have to shine for anyone.

It just is.

Quiet. Steady. Whole.

With every breath, feel it glow a little brighter.

Let it lift your spirits.

And remind you that you are already enough.

Sit with this light for a few minutes.

Let it keep glowing—just for you.

THE RICE LEAF

The monk searched every scroll and sutra, every whispered word between bells, for something deeper.

He chased insights like fireflies—always just out of reach.

One morning, the master called him over.

Without a word, he placed a single grain of rice on the monk's open palm.

"Look closely," he said.

The monk leaned in.

The grain was pale. Slightly curved. A tiny crack along its back.

Then a breeze came—soft, uncertain—and lifted it away.

The monk watched it drift upward and vanish.

He did not speak.

He had nothing to ask.

REFLECTION

When was the last time you truly noticed something small?

____

____

____

____

ZEN QUOTE

 If you correct your mind, the rest of your life will fall into place.

LAO TZU

THE MONK BENEATH THE FLOOR

While sweeping beneath the floorboards, the youngest student found something buried in dust— an old robe, neatly folded. Stitched at the hem, a patch worn soft by years of kneeling.

No name. No record.

He brought it to the master.

She held it a moment, then brushed the dust from its sleeve.

"Some build temples with stone," she said. "Some with silence."

She placed it back beneath the floor.

The student swept slower that day.

REFLECTION

How do you build your temple: with stone, with words, or with quiet?

____
____
____
____

ZEN QUOTE

To attain knowledge, add things every day. To attain wisdom, remove things every day.

LAO TZU

home

November

THE SKY IN THE BOWL

THE MONK SAT ALONE, a bowl of water in his lap.

He had meant to wash his hands, but something caught him.

In the surface: the drifting of clouds. A bird gliding. The pale curve of the moon.

He watched, unmoving, for a long time.

When the master passed by, the monk whispered, "I think I've seen a vision."

The master glanced into the bowl, then into the monk's eyes.

"You didn't see the sky," she said.

"You saw your stillness."

REFLECTION

When your world feels full, could it be reflecting your own stillness?

____

____

____

____

ZEN QUOTE

 Become like a child — clear, open, and ready for anything.

LAMA YESHE

MINDFUL MOMENTS

Pause before answering
Let your words arrive like guests—not passengers.

THE BAMBOO THAT BENT

A storm rolled through the valley, tearing branches, splitting trunks, shifting stones from their beds.

When the winds settled, the monks walked the grounds in silence, taking in the damage.

All had been struck—except a single stalk of bamboo by the garden wall, still standing, still whole.

"Why didn't it fall?" a young monk asked.

The master touched the wet leaves.

"It did," she said.

REFLECTION

What looks like resilience in your life—but feels like surrender?

____

____

____

____

ZEN QUOTE

" Life is a balance between holding on and letting go.

RUMI

MEDITATION: THE SPACE BETWEEN SOUNDS

Type: Breath Anchor with Inner Stillness

Theme: Inner peace, presence

Close your eyes and begin to listen.

Not to the sounds themselves—

but to the spaces between them.

A pause between words.

A silence between birdsongs.

The hush before the next breath.

There is peace in those spaces.

A stillness that doesn't need to be explained.

Let your breath slow to match the quiet.

Let your body rest in that in-between place.

Stay there for a few minutes.

Let the silence between sounds hold you.

THE SILENCE BETWEEN WORDS

The student memorized everything the master said—each phrase, each pause, each parable.

He could recite whole lectures backward. He spoke the teachings as if they were his own breath.

One evening, the master handed him a cup of tea and said, "Now repeat what I did not say."

The student opened his mouth.

Then slowly closed it.

Steam rose between them.

REFLECTION

Have you ever felt more connected in silence than in conversation?

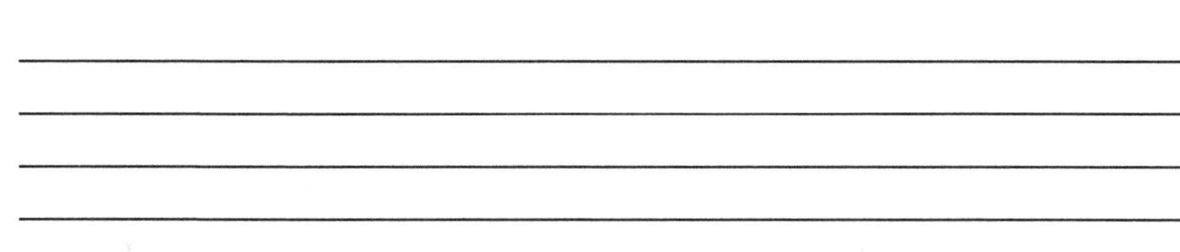

ZEN QUOTE

When you realize how perfect everything is, you will tilt your head back and laugh at the sky.

BUDDHA

THE GATE WITHOUT A PATH

In the middle of a wide, empty field stood a gate.

No fence. No walls. No road leading in or out.

A traveler came upon it and paused.

"This must be important," he thought, and waited for someone to open it.

Seasons turned. Grass grew tall around his feet.

Birds nested in the gate's frame. Still, he waited.

One morning, without thought or ceremony, he stepped around it and kept walking.

The field did not change.

But he did.

REFLECTION

What are you still waiting to begin—when nothing's really in your way?

———————————————————————————————————————
———————————————————————————————————————
———————————————————————————————————————
———————————————————————————————————————

ZEN QUOTE

> The soul always knows what to do to heal itself. The challenge is to silence the mind.

CAROLINE MYSS

THE SHADOW'S SMILE

The monk noticed his shadow during walking meditation—long, sharp, always one step behind.

He tried to outrun it with mantras, outshine it with incense, dissolve it in silence.

Still, it followed.

So he meditated longer. Chanted louder. Bowed deeper.

But the shadow remained.

One evening, as the sun dipped low, he turned to face it.

It smiled.

So did he.

Neither moved again.

REFLECTION

What part of yourself have you been trying to escape?

____

____

____

____

ZEN QUOTE

> Mindfulness isn't difficult. We just need to remember to do it.

SHARON SALZBERG

MINDFUL MOMENTS

Feel water on your skin
Cold, clean, awake. A reminder that you're alive.

THE MASTER WHO FORGOT

The hall was full. The students sat straight, ready to receive the master's most sacred teaching.

He began, voice calm, words flowing like water.

Then—he stopped.

Silence.

A flicker of confusion crossed his face. He looked at the scroll in his hands, then at the students.

"I've forgotten it," he said softly.

A gasp rippled through the hall.

The master set the scroll aside.

"Then let us sit in what remains."

And they did.

Years later, that was all they remembered.

REFLECTION

Could silence be the teaching you didn't expect—but needed?

____

____

____

____

watch

 Respond to every call that excites your spirit.

RUMI

MEDITATION: THANK YOU, BODY

Type: Body Awareness with Gratitude

Theme: Appreciation, embodiment

Close your eyes and bring your attention to your body.

Start with your feet.

Then your legs.

Your belly.

Your hands.

Your face.

Feel each part, without judgment.

Now, offer a quiet "thank you" to your body.

For carrying you.

For breathing for you.

For feeling, sensing, and healing.

No matter how it looks or feels, this body is your home.

Sit with this gratitude for a few minutes.

Fully embrace this moment.

THE STONE IN THE SHOE

For days, the monk walked with a limp.

He blamed the road—too rough, too uneven, too long.

He blamed his age. His sandals. Even the weather.

But the ache grew sharper.

Finally, beneath a tree, he sat down and removed his shoe.

Inside, a single stone—no larger than a grain of rice.

He held it up to the sky and whispered,

"So it was you all along."

REFLECTION

What small thing have you been carrying that causes more pain than it seems to deserve?

____

____

____

____

ZEN QUOTE

 The way out is through.

ROBERT FROST

　　　　　　　　　　　　　　　　　KAI TSUKIMI

ease

THE MIRROR IN THE RAIN

In the temple courtyard stood a mirror—always polished, always gleaming.

Students passed by and checked their robes, their posture, their eyes.

One day, it rained.

The mirror blurred, then vanished beneath ripples.

No faces. No sky. Just water trembling in a shallow frame.

When the storm passed and the clouds broke, the master stood beside it and said,

"That was its truest reflection."

REFLECTION

Can you sit with yourself when everything feels unclear?

____

____

____

____

ZEN QUOTE

Awaken to the mystery of being here and enter the quiet immensity of your own presence.

JOHN O'DONOHUE

December

arrive

THE WIND'S ANSWER

THE STUDENT BOWED LOW.

"What is the highest teaching?" he asked.

The master said nothing.

Instead, she rose, crossed the room, and opened the window.

A gust of wind swept through—cool, sudden. It scattered the scrolls, lifted the incense smoke, rustled the flame of the lantern.

Then stillness.

The master closed the window.

The student bowed again—lower this time.

REFLECTION

Have you ever received an answer that didn't come in words?

____

____

____

____

ZEN QUOTE

Nature does not hurry, yet everything is accomplished.

LAO TZU

MINDFUL MOMENTS

Bow to the moment
It's not yesterday. It's not tomorrow. Just this—right here.

THE BOWL THAT WASN'T MISSING

One morning, a monk noticed his favorite bowl was gone.

He searched his room, the kitchen, the garden. He questioned the other monks. He skipped meals, missed prayers, retraced every step.

Sleep slipped away. Days blurred.

On the third morning, he returned to his cushion—and there it was.

The bowl. Quiet. Unmoved.

He brought it to the master in disbelief.

She glanced at it, then at him.

"It was never missing," she said.

"Only you were."

REFLECTION

What have you been searching for that might already be beside you?

____

____

____

____

ZEN QUOTE

> Do not dwell in the past, do not dream of the future, concentrate the mind on the present moment.

BUDDHA

MEDITATION: COMING HOME

Type: Visualization with Whole-Body Awareness

Theme: Wholeness, return, completion

Imagine a small warm house in the center of your chest.

A place no one else can enter—only you.

It's peaceful here.

Still. Safe.

The light is soft.

The air is quiet.

With each breath, feel yourself returning to this place.

Not to escape the world, but to come home to yourself.

Rest here for a few minutes.

Let yourself arrive fully.

You are home.

THE WRONG DOOR

A traveler arrived late for the evening sermon.

In his haste, he pushed open the wrong door.

Inside: no cushions, no altar—just silence. A few figures sat in stillness, eyes lowered, unmoving.

No one looked up. No one spoke.

So he stayed.

Hours passed. Thoughts rose, then fell away. The quiet deepened.

When he finally stood, his shoulders were lighter.

He never did find the "right" room.

REFLECTION

Could getting lost be its own kind of arrival?

____

____

____

____

root

ZEN QUOTE

 When we try to pick out anything by itself, we find it hitched to everything else in the universe.

JOHN MUIR

THE WHISPER ON THE PAGE

In the back of the library, a student found a scroll—faded, frayed, its writing nearly vanished.

He studied it for weeks, tracing the ghost of each stroke, piecing together fragments.

One evening, he brought it to the master.

"I think I've uncovered most of it," he said.

The master took the scroll, ran her fingers lightly across the page, and smiled.

"Good," she said. "Now read what it tried not to say."

REFLECTION

What have you been overlooking because it doesn't speak loudly?

ZEN QUOTE

It is not length of life, but depth of life.

RALPH WALDO EMERSON

THE FINGER

Each day, the boy followed the master.

He watched. He listened.

He saw the finger.

Whenever someone asked about awakening, the master said nothing—only lifted his finger into the still air.

One day, the boy raised his own finger to a traveler, imitating the master's silence.

The master saw.

Said nothing.

The next morning, the boy stood beside the river.

The master came up behind him—quiet as moss.

And cut off the boy's finger.

The boy screamed and turned to flee.

"Wait," the master said.

The boy turned.

The master raised a single finger.

The boy froze.

And saw nothing.

And everything.

REFLECTION

Can pain itself become a doorway?

ZEN QUOTE

Not knowing is the most intimate.

ZEN KOAN

THE MASTER'S LAUGH

The students sat under the plum tree, locked in debate.

"What is true enlightenment?" one asked.

"It's awareness beyond thought," said another.

"No, it's the absence of self," insisted a third.

Hours passed. Voices rose. Faces tightened.

Finally, they turned to the master for clarity.

He glanced at them—then burst out laughing.

Still chuckling, he pointed to the garden, where a frog sat blinking in the sun.

"That one's closer than any of you."

REFLECTION

When was the last time you laughed at your own seriousness?

____

____

____

____

ZEN QUOTE

> When we are no longer able to change a situation, we are challenged to change ourselves.

VIKTOR E. FRANKL

touch

THE CLOCK WITHOUT HANDS

In the meditation hall, a clock hung above the altar.

It had no hands. No ticking sound. No numbers.

Just a pale face, empty and still.

One day, a new student asked, "Why keep a broken clock in a sacred space?"

The teacher smiled.

"It's the only one that's never wrong."

REFLECTION

What if you stopped measuring time so precisely—what would you notice?

____

____

____

____

ZEN QUOTE

If you understand, things are just as they are. If you do not understand, things are just as they are.

ZEN KOAN

THE BELL ROPE BREAKS

Each morning, before the sun rose, the monk rang the temple bell.

Three steady chimes. Always the same.

One morning, as he pulled, the rope snapped.

The bell stayed silent.

He reached for the spare rope—then stopped.

In the hush that followed, he heard something new:

Birdsong. Leaves brushing the eaves. His own breath, rising and falling like waves.

He never fixed the rope.

No one asked him to.

REFLECTION

When something breaks, do you rush to fix it—or wait to hear what else is there?

____

____

____

____

 If you want others to be happy, practice compassion. If you want to be happy, practice compassion.

DALAI LAMA

A Message From the Author

Thank you for taking the time to read *The Gift of Mindfulness*. My hope is that these stories have brought you moments of stillness, clarity, or even a small shift in perspective.

This book is part of a larger journey—to share the wisdom of Zen in a simple, accessible way so that more people can experience its teachings and find peace in their lives. In a world that often feels chaotic, even a single story can be a stepping stone to stillness.

If you found value in this book, I'd really appreciate it if you could leave an honest review. Your feedback helps others discover these teachings.

<u>Scan the QR Code or click here to share your thoughts.</u>

Thank you for being part of this journey.

— *Kai*

References

Books:

Hoffmann, Y. (Trans.). (1977). *Every end exposed: The 100 koans of Master Kidō with the answers of Hakuin-Zen*. Autumn Press.

Kapleau, P. (1989). *The three pillars of Zen: Teaching, practice, and enlightenment*. Anchor Books.

Morse, M. (Trans.). (2019). *The gateless gate: The classic book of Zen koans*. Counterpoint.

Reps, P., & Senzaki, N. (1957). *101 Zen stories*. Tuttle Publishing.

Reps, P., & Senzaki, N. (1998). *Zen flesh, Zen bones: A collection of Zen and pre-Zen writings*. Tuttle Publishing.

Sekida, K. (2005). *Zen training: Methods and philosophy*. Shambhala Publications.

Suzuki, S. (2006). *Zen mind, beginner's mind*. Shambhala Publications.

Watts, A. (1957). *The way of Zen*. Vintage Books.

Yamada, K. (2015). *Zen: The authentic gate*. Wisdom Publications.

Websites:

Resilient Stories. (2025, July 31). *70+ Zen quotes that will help you find inner peace*. https://resilientstories.com/zen-quotes/

Wisdom Quotes. (2025, July 31). *470 Zen quotes that will blow your mind*. https://wisdomquotes.com/zen-quotes/

Zenful Spirit. (2019, October 10). *Zen quotes to guide you to peace, clarity and enlightenment*. https://zenfulspirit.com/2019/10/10/zen-quotes/